TURTLE MOVES HOUSE

Written by Sue Graves

Illustrated by Trevor Dunton

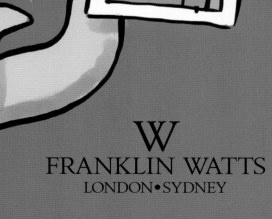

W
FRANKLIN WATTS
LONDON • SYDNEY

Turtle lived by the swamp. She lived there with her mum, dad, brother and sister. She thought it was the nicest place to live in the **whole world**.

Best of all, she lived next door to Bear.
Bear was a **good friend.**

One day, Mum and Dad said they had some **exciting news**. They said they were all moving house to the other side of the swamp.

They said there would be **more space** to play,
and they would make lots of **new friends**, too.

Turtle's brother and sister were **excited**.
But Turtle wasn't excited at all. She was **worried**.
What if she didn't like the new house? What if
she didn't like her new room? What if she didn't
want more space? She thought there was plenty of
space where she lived now!

Then Turtle thought about all her friends.
She would **miss them** very much. Worst of all,
she would miss Bear. She didn't want to **move
away** from her.

Turtle worried about making new friends.
What if she didn't make any at all?
That would be **very sad**!

Turtle went to see Bear. She told Bear all her worries. Bear said she would always be Turtle's friend wherever she lived. She said she would still see her at school.

Bear's mum said she would make lots of new friends because she was a very friendly turtle. She said she just had to take a **deep breath**, **be brave** and ask others to play. She said that was a **good way** to make friends.

Then Bear's mum said she **worried** about moving house when she was a little bear. She worried about missing all her friends. Then she had a **good idea**. She took **lots of photos** of her friends. She put the photos up in her new room. It made her new room look really special!

Bear's mum said she talked to her friends in lots of different ways. She said it helped to keep in touch! She said they visited each other as often as they could, too.

Turtle had a think. She said she could do all those things. Bear's mum said that was a good idea.

Soon moving day arrived. The new house was much bigger and there was a lot of space to play. Turtle liked her new room, but she **missed her friends**.

Turtle remembered what Bear's mum said. She put up **lots of photos**. They made her room look even better! She **chatted to her friends** on the phone and showed them her new room. She felt much happier.

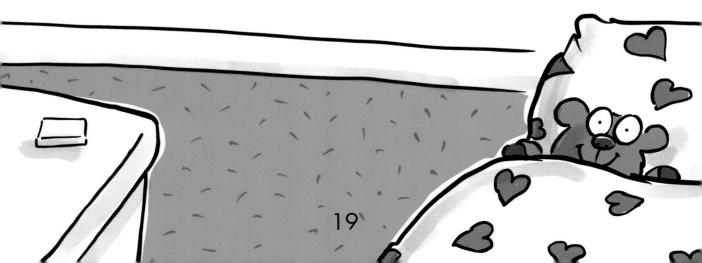

One day, though, Turtle **felt lonely**.
Everyone was playing outside.
She wanted to play,
but she didn't know anyone.

Then Turtle remembered what Bear's mum said.
She went outside. She took a **deep breath**.

She asked if she could play, too. Everyone said
yes! Soon Turtle had made lots of **new friends**.

A little later, Mum said she had a **surprise** for Turtle. She said she could have a **party** and invite her old friends. Best of all, she could invite her new friends, too.

24

Everyone came to the party. Everyone **played together**. It was the best party ever.

Turtle said it was lovely to have lots of **old friends**. She said it was lovely to make lots of **new friends**. Everyone agreed!

A note about sharing this book

The *Experiences Matter* series has been developed to provide a starting point for further discussion on how children might deal with new experiences. It provides opportunities to explore ways of developing coping strategies as they face new challenges.
The series is set in the jungle with animal characters reflecting typical behaviour traits and attitudes often seen in young children.

Turtle Moves House
This story looks at some of the things children might worry about if they are to move to a new area. It offers opportunities for them to discuss ways in which they could help themselves to settle in a new location.

How to use the book
The book is designed for adults to share with either an individual child, or a group of children, and as a starting point for discussion.

The book also provides visual support and repeated words and phrases to build reading confidence.

Before reading the story
Choose a time to read when you and the children are relaxed and have time to share the story.

Spend time looking at the illustrations and talk about what the book might be about before reading it together.

Encourage children to employ a phonics-first approach to tackling new words by sounding the words out.

After reading, talk about the book with the children:

- Ask the children to recall some of Turtle's concerns on hearing that she and her family are to move house.

- Have any of the children moved house? What things worried them? Did they worry about losing their old friends? Did they worry about the new house? Were they very attached to their old house? On the other hand, were they excited about moving? Why?

- Do the children think Bear's mum's idea of putting up photos of friends is a good way to make a room seem more familiar?

- What different ways can the children suggest to help them keep in touch with old friends? Examples might be to phone them, to send postcards if they go on holiday, to text them or to email them. Point out that even a short message can remind a friend that you are thinking of them.

Encourage the children to share their experiences. Remind all the children to listen quietly while others are speaking and to wait for their own turn to speak.

- Place the children into pairs and ask each child in the pair to send a short message of friendship to the other.

- At the end of the session, select children to show their messages to the others and use the children's work to trigger further discussion.

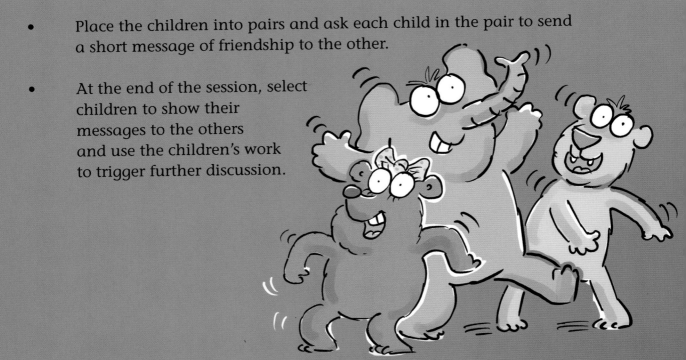

For Isabelle, William A, William G, George, Max, Emily, Leo, Caspar, Felix, Tabitha, Phoebe, Harry and Libby –S.G.

Franklin Watts
First published in 2023 by
Hodder & Stoughton

Text © Hodder & Stoughton Limited, 2023
Illustrations © Trevor Dunton, 2023

The right of Trevor Dunton to be identified as the illustrator
of this Work has been asserted in accordance with the
Copyright, Designs and Patents Act, 1988.

Editor: Jackie Hamley
Designer: Cathryn Gilbert

A CIP catalogue record for this book is available
from the British Library.

ISBN 978 1 4451 8212 4 (hardback)
ISBN 978 1 4451 8213 1 (paperback)
ISBN 978 1 4451 8873 7 (ebook)

Printed in China

Franklin Watts
An imprint of
Hachette Children's Books,
Part of Hodder & Stoughton
Carmelite House
50 Victoria Embankment
London EC4Y 0DZ

An Hachette UK company
www.hachettechildrens.co.uk

FSC
www.fsc.org

MIX
Paper from
responsible sources
FSC® C104740